No More Cheese

ISBN 978-1-64003-540-9 (Paperback)
ISBN 978-1-64003-541-6 (Digital)

First Edition

Covenant Books, Inc.
11661 Hwy 707
Murrells Inlet, SC 29576
www.covenantbooks.com

No More Cheese

Colette Ivanov

illie Mouse was in her house, contemplating food for her tea.

She opened her cupboards, and to her dismay, all she saw was cheese!

Now quite a selection she did have from Cheddar to Monterey,

But Millie was so tired of cheese, for she ate it every day.

“I can not take it,” she said out loud. “My menu has to change.”

So she sat at her table with a pen in hand for a plan she had to arrange.

MOM
AND HER PIE
TOMMY
AND HIS SANDWHICH
DAD
AND HIS FRUITS

Millie knew the house she shared with the human folk was quite big,

And several of them ate several foods that she thought she would possibly dig.

So the plan was created and designed to try a food from each folk,

And in its place she would put some cheese along with a thank-you note.

First on her list was Mom herself, who always had delectable treats.

Millie carefully made her way to find her first new food to eat.

Mom had just baked a pie, and it was sitting out to cool.

Millie poked a hole in the pie and ate the filling with her spoon.

Dear Mom,
Thank you for the pie
I really enjoyed it so
I have left some cheese in its place
And now I have to go,
Sincerely,
Millie Mouse

Millie thought this was just grand and ate up all but the pan.

She filled the pan with gouda cheese and left a note to explain.

Dear Mom,

Thank you for the pie
I really enjoyed it so
I have left some cheese in its place
And now I have to go.

Sincerely,
Millie Mouse

Peanut B
Jelly

When Tommy came home from school, he made a sandwich for a snack.

He quickly ran up to his room, but the sandwich was gone when he got back!

Millie Mouse had loaded up in her little wagon, don't you know,

And taken it off to her room so she could eat it nice and slow.

!
Dear Tommy:
Thank you for the
It was delectable
I have left some
And now I have

But to her word, she didn't forget. Tommy was left with cheddar instead,

And a little note placed on top. Tommy read what the note had said:

Dear Tommy,

Thank you for the sandwich
It was delectable, don't you know
I have left some cheese in its place
And now I have to go.

Sincerely,
Millie Mouse

Later on that night, Dad was asleep in his chair.

Millie Mouse spotted a plate of fruit, and on top was a delicious pear.

Millie mouse rolled it off, and it landed behind the chair.

Millie proceeded to have a feast of this pear right then and there!

Dad woke with a start and quickly looked around.

A piece of cheese was propped on the fruit, and a note was on the ground.

Dear Dad,

Thank you for the scrumptious pear
I couldn't just eat it slow
I have left some cheese in its place
And now I surely have to go.

Sincerely,
Millie Mouse

The next morning at breakfast time, they all compared their notes,

And figured something had to be done, so they decided to take a vote.

“All in favor that Millie should stay and join our family meals,

Raise their hands in the air.” It was a unanimous appeal.

THANK you For the Cheese
We enjoyed it very MUCH
Can you please join our table?
AND Have your Meals With us?
Sincerely,
TOMMy, MOM and Dad

So this time, they wrote a note and addressed it to Millie Mouse.

Dear Millie Mouse,

Thank you for the cheese
We enjoyed it very much
Can you please join our table
And have your meals with us?

Sincerely,
Tommy, Mom and Dad

So from then on out, there was a fourth table setting set,

And Millie Mouse brought the cheese, and they all shared the rest.

About the Author

Colette Ivanov is a marketing professional and loves to read and write in her spare time. This is her first published picture book. She was born in England but grew up in Georgia. She lives in Florida with her husband and two children.

CPSIA information can be obtained
at www.ICGtesting.com
Printed in the USA
LVHW051126211118
597736LV00006B/105